The BFF Sisters

Jennah's New Friends
A story of what true friendship is all about.

The BFF Sisters

Jennah's New Friends

A story of what true friendship is all about.

Narrated by Suzy Ismail

amana publications

First Edition
(1422AH/2001AC)
© Copyright 1422AH/2001AC
amana publications
10710 Tucker Street
Beltsville, Maryland 20705-2223 USA
Tel: (301) 595-5777 / Fax: (301) 595-5888
E-mail: amana@igprinting.com
Website: www.amana-publications.com

Library of Congress Cataloging-in-Publication Data

Ismail, Suzy.
  The BFF sisters : Jennah's new friends / narrated by Suzy Ismail.
    p. cm.
  Summary: Forming a new club to study the hadeeth with her Muslim friends
in Matawan, New Jersey, helps calm Jennah's anger when she believes a new
girl is replacing her as Yasmeen's best friend.
  ISBN 1-59008-005-X
  [1. Muslims--Fiction. 2. Best friends. 3. Friendship--Fiction. 4. Clubs--Fiction.
  5. Hadeeth--Fiction. 6. New Jersey --Fiction.] I. Title.

PZ7.18383 Bf2001
[Fic]--dc21

                                                                    2001055972

Printed in the United States of America by
International Graphics
10710 Tucker Street
Beltsville, Maryland 20705-2223   USA
Tel: (301) 595-5999 Fax: (301) 595-5888
Website: igprinting.com
E-mail: ig@igprinting.com

Bismillah Al-Rahman Al-Raheem

CHAPTER

1

"Fatimah. Cut it out! Mamma! Fatimah keeps smearing chocolate all over the floor and her clothes and her hair and... ewwww! Gross! She just put her sticky hands all over me too!!!"

I couldn't believe how disgusting my three-year-old sister was being. She was hiding under the table with an itty-bitty piece of chocolate that I'd snuck into her mouth to keep her quiet. Who would've thought that a little kid could make such a big mess out of a tiny Hershey's Kiss?

"Oooh...Fatimah! You're going to get in sooooo much trouble!" I said. "Mamma just finished cleaning up this kitchen!"

Even though I love my little sister, she can really be a pain sometimes...especially when she tries to act cute in front of all my friends by singing her corny preschool songs or when she scribbles all over my homework with her crayons. Sometimes I don't mind playing with her, but most of the time she's just a short and chubby ball of trouble.

I rolled my eyes just thinking about the fact that in a few months time I'd have to deal with another new baby brother or sister.

"What's the matter Jennah? Why do you keep screaming like that?" Mamma called from upstairs.

My mom carefully made her way down the stairs with her usual expression of worry on her face. She's really the most wonderful person in the world, but she spends a lot of time worrying. I think it's because Baba usually isn't around much.

Baba has this really important job in some big company so he's always traveling to different parts of the world. Sometimes he brings me and Fatimah cool presents like little teacups from Russia and paper fans from China. Even though the presents are nice, once in a while I wish that Baba could take me and Mamma and even Fatimah with him on one of his trips. Then again, sometimes I just wish he wouldn't have to go on those trips at all and that he could stay here instead and take us to the park or come watch me recite Qur'an in the Sunday school competitions.

"Jennah! Fatimah!" My mom shouted. "What happened to my kitchen?"

Mamma looked really angry now. She bent down under the table with her big baby-belly and scooped Fatimah off the floor.

"Ya Allah! Fatimah! What have you done to yourself?"

Just as Mamma started to get a really angry expression on her face, Fatimah lifted up her chocolate-coated lips and gave her a big, sticky kiss on the nose. All of a sudden, Mamma's anger seemed to melt away and she started to laugh.

I couldn't believe it! I thought Fatimah was going to be in big trouble for making such a mess.

I pursed my lips, shook my head, and said, "Mamma, how can you laugh right now? Don't you see what Fatimah did and what a huge mess she's made?" I wanted to make sure that Fatimah wouldn't get off the hook so easily this time.

"Oh, it's ok, Jennah. Your sister's still a little girl. She looks so funny with such a mess all over the place. She didn't mean to be bad. Anyway, aren't you the one who gave her that piece of chocolate?" Mamma asked.

"Yeah, I gave her the chocolate to keep her quiet while I practiced my part for the Sunday school play. How was I supposed to know she'd make such a mess?"

"Come on, Jennah. You know that I always tell you not to give your sister any kind of candy or sweets before lunch. You're the oldest... you should know better than that! Help me clean up this mess now, then you can give your sister a bath."

How could this be happening? I wondered. Fatimah made the mess, but I'm the one that has to clean it up!

Now, Fatimah was just sitting on the floor blowing bubbles out of her mouth, giggling as if she had just won a prize or something.

"Mamma, it's not fair! Why do I always have to do everything around the house while she just sits around and plays? I wish Baba were here! He would never make me clean up after Fatimah!" I cried.

As soon as I said those words, I knew that I wanted to take them back. Mamma's eyes started to fill with tears and even Fatimah stopped playing and looked up at me with a sad frown. I felt terrible but I didn't know what to do. I ran upstairs into my room and closed the door behind me.

With a sigh, I sat on the soft bed in my bedroom and started to cry. I curled up into a ball and hugged one of the pink, ruffled pillows that match the walls in my room. Just being in my quiet room, away from Fatimah, I felt my anger begin to fade.

I felt awful about what I had said, because I knew that it was really wrong of me to upset Mamma. It was just that I didn't know how to control myself when I got really angry. All morning I had been thinking about Baba and wishing that he were here today. Fatimah's mess just seemed to make everything worse.

It was a beautiful summer day, and I knew that all my friends were going to spend the morning with their families praying *salat al-fajr* at the Jersey beach. Afterward, they would have a huge picnic breakfast, and all of the fathers would play volleyball. The mothers would sit around, talk, and watch the little children splashing in the water or building sandcastles. I could just imagine all the other girls my age, like Yasmeen, Rahma, and Khadija, walking along the shore and talking about all the cool stuff they'd do when they went back to school in September, *insha'Allah*. I felt so left out that all of my closest friends would be having such a good time with each other while I was stuck at home.

When I told Mamma about the beach trip she told me that I could go with one of the other girls. But, when I said that it would be too embarrassing for me to go without my family, she said that she couldn't go because it would be too long of a drive for her. Then she said that she just didn't have the energy to run after Fatimah all day.

Of course, I would never go to the beach picnic alone when all my other friends would be there with their parents and brothers and sisters. It was so unfair! Everyone else except for me got to go and do fun stuff with their families all the time. I was the only one who was always disappointed and just had to deal with it.

I felt myself getting angry again, so I started to recite the Sunday school prayer that's supposed to keep shaytan away. Over and over again I kept saying "*As-staghfur Allah Al-'atheem, as-staghfur Allah Al-'atheem,*" until I started to feel a little better.

Just as I was thinking about going downstairs to apologize to Mamma, the phone rang.

I jumped off my bed and grabbed the phone off the hook. "*As-salamu 'alaikum,*" I said.

"*Wa 'alaikum as-salam,*" answered the voice on the other end. "Hey Jennah! It's me, Yasmeen. Where were you today? We had a really good time. You should've come."

I was so happy to hear from my best friend, Yasmeen, that I completely forgot what I had been angry about a few seconds earlier.

Even though Yasmeen lives down the street from me, and is also going into the sixth grade, we go to different schools. Yasmeen goes to an Islamic school almost an hour away from her house, but I go to Valley Hills, a public school that is right around the corner.

"Oh, it's okay, Yasmeen," I said. "Maybe I'll come next time, *insha'Allah*. Mamma wasn't feeling too well today."

While I was talking to Yasmeen, I realized how silly I had been acting. Of course, there would always be a next time, *insha'Allah*. Maybe, by then Baba would be here and we could all go together like all the other families.

"Oh, that's right! It's almost time for the baby to come," Yasmeen said. "Are you excited?"

Yasmeen was always bubbly and excited about everything that was going on.

"Yeah, I guess so," I answered. "But, the baby won't be here for another three months still so it seems like a long time away. Anyway, what are you doing the rest of today *insha'Allah?"* I asked, hoping Yasmeen was free, and that we might be able to go bike riding or something.

"Nothing really. Why don't you come over today? There's this new girl that I met at the mosque last week. Her name is Mariam. Her family just moved in the old house across the street from us, and she's going to be in sixth grade at my school next year, *insha'Allah*. She's really nice, so I asked her to come over for a little while today and hang out with me. You wanna' come?"

"Sure," I answered. "I'll have to ask Mamma first, of course, and I have to give my little sister a bath. But when I'm finished, I'll come over if it's okay with my mom."

Even though I wanted to go to Yasmeen's house, I was starting to get this funny feeling in my stomach when I thought about Mariam being there.

"Great, I'll call Rahma and Khadija and tell them to come over too," Yasmeen said. "Oh, wait, my mom's calling me. Hold on a sec." Yasmeen put the phone down and started speaking very quickly in Urdu to her mom.

Even though Yasmeen's family is from Pakistan and my family is from Egypt, we still get along great with each other. Sometimes I try to teach her some Arabic words and she tries to teach me Urdu.

"Alright Jennah, sorry about that. My mom was just saying that she wants you all to stay over for lunch if that's okay with you."

"Sounds good," I answered. "I'll call you later and let you know whether or not I'm allowed to come." I still couldn't shake off that bad feeling that I was having about the new girl.

"Oh, I can't wait. This is going to be so much fun," Yasmeen said. "I know you're going to love Mariam when you meet her. Talk to you later. *As-salamu 'alaikum.*"

"Wa 'alaikum as-salam."

As I hung up the phone I couldn't stop wondering why Yasmeen was so excited about Mariam. It was as if she had found a new best friend or something. I quickly tossed aside that idea and laughed nervously at the thought of Yasmeen having a new best friend. Of course she wouldn't do that to me. We had been best friends since we were little kids. She would never stop being friends with me just because a new girl had moved into town.

Pushing aside my silly thoughts, I skipped downstairs and looked for Mamma so that I could apologize for the way I had acted. I found her lying down on the couch in our cramped living room with a warm cloth on her forehead. Fatimah was playing quietly, for once, in the corner with her blocks. But, as soon as she saw me she started jumping up and down and screeching "Jen-dah! Jen-dah!"

Mamma woke up startled from her nap and looked around in panic.

"I'm sorry Mamma," I said. "I didn't mean to wake you up. I just came downstairs to give Fatimah a bath and help you clean up the kitchen a little bit. I didn't realize that you were sleeping."

My mom gave me a little smile and opened up her arms wide, but before I could move in and hug Mamma in return, Fatimah's speedy little legs carried her straight into her lap. She showered her with kisses and began her sing-song chant of "I wuv you Mommy! I wuv you Mommy!"

Rather than getting angry again about my pesky little sister's antics, I dropped a kiss on Mamma's head and hugged them both as best as I could.

"I'm sorry I said those mean things, Mamma," I said. "I know it was wrong of me to act like that and I'll try not to do it again, *insha'Allah.*"

Mamma's smile stretched into a grin as she slid Fatimah off her lap and patted the sofa next to her. I cuddled close to her as Fatimah crawled into my lap this time.

"I have a surprise for you girls. I just called your father in Malaysia and he said he might be coming home in time for your Sunday school play, *insha'Allah.* I know it's hard for you not having Baba around all the time, but we have to have patience and know that soon Allah (swt) will reward us in a way that's best for us all."

Mamma smiled, "Now, why don't you go meet up with your friends, Jennah, and I'll take care of our little monkey's mess?"

I gave my mom a big hug.

"No way," I said. "After the way I acted, I'm definitely not going out until I help you a little. I'll give Fatimah a bath while you take care of the kitchen. Then, if it's okay with you, I want to go to Yasmeen's house for lunch because her mom invited me and Rahma and Khadija over."

"I know. Yasmeen's mom just gave me a call. That's fine but try not to make too much of a mess while you are there," Mamma answered.

"I go too! I go too! I want go too with Meen and Jen-dah!" Fatimah started wailing as soon as the words were out of Mamma's mouth.

"No, no, little one. You're going to stay right here with me today," Mamma said.

"No, it's okay Mamma. I'll give her a bath and take her with me. She can play with Mustafa and Mona."

Surprisingly, Yasmeen's younger brother and sister are always happy to play with Fatimah. Although I could never understand it, I guess some kids that age think Fatimah is actually fun to be around.

"This way, Mamma, you can rest a little bit while we're gone," I said. "But, Fatimah, you have to promise you'll be a good girl. No biting or kicking or fighting with the other kids. Okay?"

I knew that Mamma must've known how guilty I was feeling for the way I had acted, since I was actually willing to take Fatimah with me to my friend's house.

"Fa-tee-ma be good. I be good good good girl, Jen-dah. I pe-rah-meese."

"Okay, then let's go take your bath now," I laughed.

Even I couldn't resist Fatimah when she wore that baby sweet innocent expression on her face.

About an hour later Fatimah was fresh and clean and we were ready to go. I grabbed her hand and we began walking down the hill towards Yasmeen's house.

CHAPTER

2

Although the walk to Yasmeen's house usually takes me only about five minutes when I'm alone, it took us over twenty minutes today because of Fatimah's dilly-dallying. By the time we reached the large two-story brick house, I was back to being a hundred percent annoyed at my little sister.

I looked around at the familiar neighborhood and thought about all the fun things that the girls and I could do today. A smile immediately lit up my face as a million great ideas started to crowd into my mind.

At the sound of the neighbor's dog barking, I quickly snapped out of my trance and turned to give Fatimah one last warning about proper behavior before ringing Yasmeen's doorbell. But, when I turned, I realized that my little sister was gone!

"Fatimah! Fatimah! Where are you?" I called. "This is no time for games. Get back here right now or else I'm sending you home!"

I waited impatiently on the doorstep, sure that at any minute Fatimah would come bounding through the bushes with a naughty grin on her face. I waited and waited and waited. But still, there was no sign of Fatimah.

Mumbling to myself, I started looking everywhere for her.

At first, all I could think about was how I would tell Mamma when I found her, and how she'd be sure to get punished. But, as the minutes began to tick by and there was still no sign of Fatimah, I started to really worry.

I began to think, What if something happened to Fatimah? What if someone had kidnapped her while my back was turned? What if she had fallen into a hole in the ground and had broken her leg and was lying there in pain waiting for someone to save her? What if I never found Fatimah and had to go back home without her? What if....

I couldn't stop the bad thoughts from coming into my head, and I found myself praying to Allah that my little sister would be okay. Over and over I kept whispering to myself, "Ya, Allah! Please let Fatimah be okay. I promise I'll be nice to her from now on. Please, ya Allah, let her be okay."

As I wiped away the tears from my eyes, I suddenly heard a sound coming from Yasmeen's backyard. I ran to the back of the house, tripping over Mustafa's swing-set and Mona's scattered toys.

"Jen-dah! Jen-dah! Where you are Jen-dah?" Fatimah called out in her cheerful voice. "You was hiding Jen-dah and I find you!"

I picked myself up off the ground and couldn't believe what I saw. There, in a huge mud-puddle in the middle of the backyard, Fatimah was happily splashing around without a care in the world. Her once clean hair was filled with mud and her pudgy little face was covered with dirt. The white dress that I had dressed her in was now a terrible shade of brown and her dirty little hands were busy making mud pies.

I stood rooted to my spot for a few moments until I could finally get my mouth moving again. I was about to let Fatimah really have it, when suddenly I saw one of her mud pies arcing through the sky and heading right towards me. I tried to duck, but it was too late. The mud pie landed right in the middle of my face!

The first thought that flashed through my mind before my

anger could catch up with my surprise was that Fatimah had really good aim.

At that moment, the back door opened and Mustafa and Mona, Yasmeen's twin brother and sister, came rushing out to join in the fun. Rahma, Khadija, Yasmeen, and her mom quickly followed the twins into the backyard while the new girl came up behind them.

I couldn't believe how embarrassed I was. My face was covered with mud and my little sister, the pest, looked like the abominable dirt midget. I could've just died on the spot.

Instead of the shrieks of horror that I expected to hear, everyone just burst into laughter at the same time. I think the screams would have been better. Yasmeen's mom quickly took charge of the situation by pulling out the hose and washing up Fatimah, who, of course, was wiggling with delight at the chance to get sprayed with water while fully clothed. I, on the other hand, stayed glued to my spot in the hopes that the ground would just open up and swallow me.

Yasmeen's mom looked over at me and said, "Oh, Jennah. It looks like you've had a long day today. Why don't you go inside with the girls? Wash up and make *wudu'* for *salat al-dhuhr* while I take care of Fatimah and try to find her something dry to wear from Mona's closet."

I nodded numbly and started heading towards the door.

"*Masha'Allah*, your sister is soooo cute, Jennah! I wish I had a little sister like that," said the new girl.

While Mariam was busy oohing and aahing over my little sister, I shot her a look that could have melted steel.

Sensing my quick temper, Yasmeen grabbed my arm and pushed me towards the house. She said, "Come on, Jennah. Let's all make *wudu'* and pray together and then we can go upstairs and hang out a little. I have so much cool stuff to tell you about."

After blowing all the mud out of my nose, washing up, and praying, I headed upstairs to join the other girls in Yasmeen's bedroom.

As soon as I walked into Yasmeen's room I started to feel better. Her room is very pink, just like mine, but it's much smaller and cozier. She has these huge pillows thrown all over her thick carpet so wherever you sit you sink into unbelievable softness. Her walls are decorated with different *surahs* from the Qur'an and her little kitten, Kit-Cat, loves to cuddle at the foot of her bed.

No matter how much I beg Mamma for a kitten, she always says no because she's allergic to any kind of animal and Fatimah would probably strangle or suffocate any pet we ever got anyway.

The thought of Fatimah brought me back to reality and I realized that Yasmeen was talking, "So, like I was telling you Jennah, this is Mariam. She lives across the street. Her family moved to North Jersey from Palestine a few years ago and now they decided to move here. Mariam was just saying how she wished she had a younger brother or sister like Fatimah because she only has one older sister in college right now just like Rahma's sisters. I told her she was lucky."

As Yasmeen was going through her long introduction, I looked Mariam over closely. I noticed right away that she was about my height, not too tall and not too short. But she was also much thinner and seemed a lot taller because she was so thin.

Although I used to think that one day my baby fat would somehow disappear, I now realize that my chipmunk cheeks are probably here for good. Looking at Mariam, I couldn't help but feel a little jealous of how pretty she was.

Mariam's long brown hair came down in soft waves to her waist and was almost as long as Rahma's. The rest of her features seemed to be just as beautiful as her hair. Khadija and I wear our hair in really short curls since it's just easier to comb that way, while Yasmeen wears *hijab*. She is the only one from our group of friends who wears *hijab* in school and outside of school...the rest of us talk about it a lot and hope to start wearing it soon *insha'Allah*.

I looked around the room at all my friends and couldn't help but compare how different we all were.

Since Khadija is African American and her parents don't speak Arabic at home, she's trying really hard to learn the language at Sunday school to help her in reading the Qur'an. Khadija has always been the real tomboy of the group, coming up with adventurous games to play and wild things to do even when we were kids.

Rahma's personality is the complete opposite of Khadija's, which is probably why they get along so well together. Rahma comes from an Afghanistani background, but her family has been in America for so long that they don't really call Afghanistan "back home" anymore the way my parents still talk about Egypt. She's usually very shy and withdrawn in front of grown-ups or new people. But, when it's just the gang, Rahma's the sweetest and most talkative person around.

Yasmeen and I have always been the best of friends too, even though we're really different. Yasmeen's always real careful about what she says, and tries to make sure everyone is happy all of the time, while I can be a little bossy sometimes and I have a hard time controlling my temper when I get angry. It's something I really am trying to work on.

"Earth to Jennah! Earth to Jennah! Jennah, what are you thinking about? You totally zoned out!" Khadija was waving her arms in front of my face and snapping her fingers as if she was trying to shake me out of a trance.

"Oh. I'm sorry guys. I didn't mean to daze off like that," I said. "I guess I'm just really tired from Fatimah's tricks all day today. So, what's new with everyone?"

"Khadija was just telling us about another new girl who moved close to her house. Her name is Lisa and she's going to be in sixth grade with us at Valley Hills School next year too, *insha'Allah*," Rahma answered.

"Speaking about being in the same school next year, *insha'Allah*, I'm so excited that Mariam's going to be in my Islamic school," Yasmeen chimed in. "We'll probably take the same bus together and be in all the same classes. Now when you guys talk about all the stuff that goes on in your school, Mariam and I can talk about stuff that goes on at Noor Al-Huda School."

As I listened to Yasmeen's excited voice, I felt those same fluttering feelings of jealousy in my stomach again. It wasn't fair. Why was Mariam going to go to the same school as my best friend? I could just imagine her sharing secrets with Yasmeen and calling her every night to talk about schoolwork or their teachers. Soon, Yasmeen would be so caught up with her new friend that she'd completely forget about me.

Mariam's voice snapped me back out of my bad thoughts.

"So, school doesn't start until September which is still two months away. What do you guys do all summer long to keep yourselves busy?" she asked.

"I dunno' Mariam," answered Khadija. "Usually, Yasmeen goes to Pakistan and Jennah goes to Egypt, and me and Rahma just kind of hang out all summer long and do nothing."

"I don't think we do nothing Khadija," Rahma quickly jumped in to defend herself. "I mean we go to Sunday school and help the little kids at the Muslim day camp sometimes, and well... yeah, I guess you're right, most of the time we really don't do anything too exciting." Rahma giggled and threw an overstuffed pillow at Khadija.

"Well, you know what?" Yasmeen said. "Jennah and I aren't going anywhere this summer because Jennah's mom is going to have the baby soon, *insha'Allah*, and my dad has to work all summer long so I guess we're both going to stay here and do nothing right along with you guys, then. Right, Jennah?" Yasmeen looked at me for agreement.

"Well, wait. If we're all going to be here all summer long, why don't we think of something fun that we could do," I answered.

I figured if I could come up with a great idea that would keep us busy then Yasmeen would remember how much fun I could be. Maybe then, she'd forget all about Mariam.

"I know! Why don't we start a club?" I exclaimed.

"A what? A club? Yeah, okay, whatever. C'mon now... you've got to be kidding me! We're not two years old anymore, Jennah," Khadija said. Of course, Khadija was the first to disagree. Since I expected it right away, and since I was so used to her big mouth, I didn't really mind her making fun of my idea that much.

Rahma chimed in, "Yeah, Jennah, what do you think we need a 'club' for anyway? I mean, if we did do this club thing, would we have to like sing songs or something?"

Rahma, as usual, had to be the only one to quickly side with Khadija. I'm sure that if Khadija had said she liked my idea, Rahma would have agreed with her in the same way.

"C'mon guys, give Jennah a chance to explain... maybe it really is a good idea," Yasmeen cut in.

Yasmeen, the peacemaker, was quick to help me out as usual. I looked at her and gave her a grateful smile for always being on my side.

Now that I knew that at least someone would back me up, I started talking with a little more confidence.

"Yeah, just give me a chance to tell you more about it... okay? You know this club thing could really turn out to be a lot of fun. We could make it into like a special thing where only certain people could join. We could do something really cool at each of our meetings like all those girls on TV do, or like in those books that we have to read for school sometimes. Maybe we could solve crimes, tell stories, raise money, or maybe even baby-sit." I was really starting to warm up to the idea, and I was getting more and more excited as I talked about it.

Of course, Miss 'goody two-shoes,' Mariam, had to interrupt my train of thought by saying all of a sudden, "Wait, I have an even better idea. Where I used to live, the adults used to get together once a week and talk about different hadeeths that they'd read. Each person would take a turn and read a *hadeeth* and then explain it to everyone else. That way everyone learned something new at each meeting. We could do something like that."

Khadija, of course, was shaking her head violently in disagreement.

"Oh, come on now girls!" She said. "That is the silliest thing that I've ever heard! There is no way that I am going to spend my wonderful summer vacation studying or doing any kind of work that I don't have to do just to keep you guys happy. I'd rather spend my time making mud-pies with Fatimah!"

"Khadija's right!" Rahma nodded in agreement. "We do enough Islamic stuff every Sunday at the *masjid*. Why on earth would we spend even more time doing the same stuff over again? I think I'd rather eat the mud-pies that Fatimah and Khadija will spend all summer making."

Rahma just had to agree with Khadija on everything.

Although I wasn't crazy about the thought of siding with Mariam, I have to admit that I kind of liked her idea. I've always been really interested in reading lots of books about Islam and learning more about the life of the Prophet (pbuh), and Mamma's always telling me about different *hadeeths* and *dua*'s that I should memorize. Maybe it would be fun to learn more about Islam just by talking with my friends. Of course, there was no way I would ever tell Mariam that I actually liked her idea. Instead, I just waited for Yasmeen to step in and try to defend her, as I was sure she would.

Right away, Yasmeen started backing up Mariam. "You guys are so quick to judge everyone. Come on now! Mariam just had a really good idea! It won't be like Sunday school, Rahma, because it will be just us. We'll be learning all about the life of the Prophet (pbuh) and the way a good Muslim should behave... which is something that I think we all need to learn a little more about."

"Anyway, Khadija, it's not like it would be homework or anything. It'll be fun because nobody would make us read the *hadeeths*. We'd be doing it all on our own. I think we should give it a try! What do you think, Jennah?" Yasmeen asked.

I really didn't want to answer Yasmeen, but I realized that the whole club idea pretty much rested on my shoulders right now.

"Well, I guess it could work," I said slowly. "But, because I came up with the idea of starting a club, then I have to be the first one to pick a *hadeeth* and present it next week, *insha'Allah*. I have this really good *hadeeth* book at home that Baba brought back for me from Saudia Arabia."

"You know, Khadija and Rahma, if we get together next week, *insha'Allah*, and you think the meetings are corny then we won't have to do them anymore," I said. I knew I was being bossy, but I wanted to make sure that Mariam didn't get all the credit.

I could tell that Rahma and Khadija were at least starting to consider the idea a little bit more when Rahma quietly turned to Khadija and said, "Jennah's right, Khadija. We should give it a try. After all, we really should start learning more about Islam on our own. I think we're old enough now to start reading stuff because we want to and not because we have to."

Rahma's probably the only one of us who can convince Khadija of anything. So, now that she was agreeing with me a little bit, I was sure that Khadija would soon give in.

Just as I had guessed, Khadija started to agree, "Alright, alright, alright. I guess I'm outnumbered. As long as Jennah's doing all the work for next week, *insha'Allah*, then I guess I won't mind coming."

"So, anyway, if we're gonna' go with this whole club business, then shouldn't we come up with a name and a place for us to meet or something?" Rahma asked.

"Well, a place to meet is easy," Yasmeen answered quickly. "I think we should keep meeting here in my room because Rahma shares a room with her older sister, Khadija's house is farther away and Mariam's family is still getting settled in their house. Oh, and of course, we can't use your room, Jennah, since Fatimah's moving in with you as soon as the baby's born, *insha'Allah*."

"Ahhhhh…don't even remind me, Yasmeen! I don't know what I'm going to do then!" I groaned.

"Alright, now that the meeting place is taken care of, let's come up with a name," said Rahma.

I could tell she was really starting to get into the whole idea. Her normally white cheeks were beginning to get flushed with excitement at the thought of being part of something new.

"What if we call ourselves the Best Friends Club since we're all best friends?" She suggested.

"Well, that seems a little common for a club name." Yasmeen answered, "Why don't we call ourselves The B.F.F Club? That's kind of different."

Yasmeen's eyes were already glowing at the thought of it.

"What? The BFF Club? Why would we call ourselves The BFF Club? What does BFF stand for anyway? Bald, Fat and Funny or Beautiful, Famous and Funky, or maybe Big, Fake and..."

"No, Khadija! Duh!" We all cut her off before she could get going with one of her sarcastic jokes.

"Of course it doesn't mean any of those. B.F.F is short for Best Friends Forever. I think it's a beautiful name for our club because I would really love to be friends with all of you forever," Mariam said.

Her sweetness was making me sick, but Yasmeen was just eating it up.

"Aww. That's such a nice thing to say Mariam. I think B.F.F is perfect for us, too. Hey, maybe we could call ourselves The BFF Sisters instead of the The BFF Club since we're all sisters in Islam," Yasmeen suggested.

"That's perfect, Yasmeen. We'll be The BFF Sisters!" Rahma and Mariam exclaimed, nodding their heads in excited agreement, while Khadija just shrugged.

I was feeling more and more angry by the minute. The girls just kept talking to each other as if I was invisible. I couldn't believe they didn't even care what I thought. All they could think about right now was how great Mariam's idea for a *hadeeth* club was. But, it wasn't Mariam's idea at all... it was mine!

Unable to hold in my anger any longer I broke into my friends' excited chatter. In a cool voice I said, "Well, if we are going to call ourselves The BFF Sisters then we should be sure that the only people who join the club are our true best friends."

"What do you mean, Jennah? All of us are friends here," Yasmeen said in a concerned voice.

"I mean that we don't want any new people joining our club. We've all really been best friends for as long as we can remember, so, I don't think people like Mariam should be allowed to join the club. We barely even know her."

As I looked at the shocked faces of my friends, I realized that what I had said was really mean.

For the second time today, I regretted the words that slipped out of my mouth. Just like Mamma, Mariam's eyes filled up with tears. But, instead of apologizing and trying to comfort Mariam, I ran out of Yasmeen's room, down the stairs, and out the door, without stopping to say *salam* to her mom or to even take Fatimah back home with me.

CHAPTER

3

I was almost halfway home before I had to slow down a bit to catch my breath and wipe the tears from my eyes. As I walked the rest of the way, I couldn't help thinking about what a monster I had been. I knew that what I had said to Mariam was really mean... but all day today people were being so unfair. First Fatimah kept acting up, and I knew Mamma would blame it on me, then Mariam kept acting like she was Yasmeen's new best friend, and finally all the girls at Yasmeen's house were pretending like I was invisible and that 'Miss Mariam' was just the most wonderful person alive! UGHHH! I was getting so angry again just thinking about the things that had happened to me today.

Because I was so angry, I didn't realize that I had walked right past my house and down the street. Without even thinking about it, I found myself right in front of the little mosque in my neighborhood.

The mosque is really just a small house that all the Muslim families in the area helped buy and fix up. When we first moved to Matawan, we found that the nearest mosque was about an hour away, so, all the Muslims in the community got together and built this little mosque so that we could have lectures, prayers, weekend school, and community dinners all the time.

It's especially nice during *Ramadan* when the whole community comes here to have *iftar* together.

Since I was already here and knew that it was time for *salat al-'asr*, I decided to go into the mosque and pray so that maybe I could calm my anger down a little bit before going home.

I made *wudu'* and sat waiting for the *adthan*. As the call to prayer was being made by Bilal, Khadija's older brother, I felt myself starting to calm down a little bit. I closed my eyes and recited the *dua'* I had learned to say when listening to the adthan. As it came to an end, I heard a voice whisper in my ear *"As-salamu 'alaikum."*

I looked up with a start and then suddenly a big grin spread across my face. My Sunday school teacher, Sister Iman, was standing right next to me preparing for *salah.* I gave her a quick hug and straightened my line for prayer.

After praying, Sister Iman came over to where I was sitting. "How are you, little Jennah? And how are your family and friends? Why haven't you come to visit Brother Yousef and me lately? Now that you are on summer vacation I only get to see you at the Sunday school once a week. Why don't you come have a cup of iced tea with me now?"

Sister Iman's sweet voice immediately made me feel a hundred percent better. She is probably the most beautiful person I know. She is so tall and gentle and she never raises her voice, no matter how bad we are at school. Even though it seems like she is always teaching at the *masjid* with her husband, Brother Yousef, they never get tired of us, and their house is always open to everyone all the time. Although they don't have any of their own children, I know they think of all of us as their kids and they make us feel the same way, too.

While I listened to Sister Iman asking me again to spend some time with her, I knew that she was the one that I really wanted to talk to about all the terrible things that I had done today.

"Okay," I quickly answered. "But, I have to call Mamma first because she thinks I'm still at Yasmeen's house."

"Good idea. Be sure to give her my *salams*," said Sister Iman. "You can call her from the *masjid* office phone. I'm sure Brother Yousef won't mind, *insha'Allah*," Sister Iman giggled like a schoolgirl. "When you're finished calling your mom come right over. I'm going to go on ahead of you and get started on making us some yummy iced tea."

I nodded my head and walked towards the office. Sister Iman's house is right next door to the *masjid*, which is why Brother Yousef locks up and takes care of the mosque. I dialed the number to our house and prayed that Mamma wouldn't be too angry that I had left Yasmeen's house without taking Fatimah and without telling her.

"As-salamu 'alaikum," Mamma said, picking up the phone on the first ring.

"Wa 'alaikum as-salam. It's me Mamma," I answered.

"Al-hamdu-lilah! Oh Jennah! Where have you been? I've been so worried about you. Yasmeen's mom called and said you ran out of the house without eating lunch or taking Fatimah with you. Is everything okay? Where are you now?" Mamma's worried words rushed out of her mouth all at once.

"I'm sorry Mamma. I should have called you first, but I just went to pray *salat al-'asr* in the *masjid*. Then I met Sister Iman, and she asked me to come over for a little bit. I promise, Mamma, if I can go to Sister Iman's house, then I promise, I promise, I promise, that I'll go back and pick up Fatimah, and explain to you what happened, but please, please, please can I go to Sister Iman's house for a little bit first… please?"

I stopped my rambling to take a quick breath. I figured that my mom probably didn't catch a word I had said, but I really wanted to talk to Sister Iman because I knew that she would be the one person who would understand how I was feeling.

"Oh, alright, Jennah," my mom said. "You can go for a little while… but make sure you let me know where you're going before you go anywhere else. And I want you to pick up Fatimah in about a half-hour because you know how cranky she gets if she misses her nap."

"Okay, Mamma. I promise I won't forget!"

I grinned into the phone and quickly said *salam* before hanging up.

I was feeling happier and happier by the moment. I couldn't wait to spend some time with Sister Iman. She was the only adult who I felt I could really talk to. Instead of being like a mom or a teacher or something, I always felt like she was my older sister, or like a really good friend.

I tiptoed through the *masjid* quietly and quickly made my way to Sister Iman's house.

As soon as I stepped inside the cool air-conditioned hall, I felt at home. I slipped off my shoes and called out "*As-salamu 'alaikum!*"

"Oh, Jennah, I'm in the kitchen...come right in!" Called Sister Iman.

I took a deep sniff of the yummy Libyan cookies that I knew she was just pulling out of the oven as I headed towards the cozy kitchen.

"I hope you don't mind, Jennah, but I decided to make us some lemonade instead of iced tea to go with these cookies I baked," Sister Iman said as she smiled at me from behind the kitchen counter.

"Of course I don't mind," I answered as I hopped onto a high stool. "I love lemonade!" I mumbled between mouthfuls of delicious cookies.

"Well then, be sure to say *bismillah* and drink up."

Sister Iman put a tall glass of icy lemonade right next to the plate of warm cookies and sat down beside me.

As I polished off the last drops of my drink and munched on a few more cookies, I noticed that Sister Iman was sitting very quietly next to me, just waiting for me to clear my mind and start talking to her.

"There now, Jennah. Do you feel a little better?" She asked me with concern in her voice. "You looked kind of upset before in the *masjid*."

I swallowed the last crumbs in my mouth and smiled at my friend. She always seemed to know exactly when I needed to talk.

"Well, I was upset. But, now I feel better," I said. "See, I did something really mean today to this new girl named Mariam, who just moved in across from Yasmeen's house."

"Ah, yes... Mariam.... I met her this morning at the beach picnic. She's a very nice girl. Why would you be mean to her? You're always so friendly to everyone. It doesn't seem like you to be mean to someone new," Sister Iman questioned gently with a puzzled look.

"I know it was wrong of me, but I told her that I didn't want to be friends with her and that she couldn't join our *hadeeth* club. I didn't really mean to hurt her...it's just that I got so angry because Yasmeen was acting like Mariam was her new best friend. And everyone else kept on saying how cool she was and how much I was going to love her. But, I didn't love her... she just really annoyed me, and then I kind of exploded in front of all the other girls. Now I'm sure that everyone hates me." The words just rushed out, and the tears sprang to my eyes again as I remembered the things that had happened earlier on today.

"Silly, Jennah! I'm sure your friends don't hate you. I mean what you did definitely was not very nice, but I think you already know that since you regret saying the mean things that you did. But, since you can't go back in time and change what happened, you just have to think of what you can do in the future, *insha'Allah*, to make it up to your friends. Sitting around being depressed and wishing you could take back your words is really not going to help you in any way," Sister Iman said as she patted my back and looked at me understandingly.

"You know Jennah, it's hard sometimes when you love a friend very much, and you feel like you might lose that friend because of someone else. But, as Muslims we have to understand what friendship is all about. We have to try as much as possible to control our anger and share our feelings with each other, rather than just running away every time we face a problem. I think you know exactly the right thing to do, but you're just putting it off a little."

"Yeah, I know you're right," I answered. "But, it's so hard to apologize."

"Well, you're almost grown up now, and only you know what you have to do." Sister Iman shrugged gently and began putting the empty cookie plates into the kitchen sink.

As I sat there, I thought about what she had said for a moment. Then, I decided that I really did know the one thing that I had to do right away.

I smiled at Sister Iman because I could tell that she knew me really well. "Actually, I know I have to do a lot more than just apologize.... I have to really try to control my anger and jealousy from now on, or else I really will wind up having no friends at all. You know what? I'm going to go back to Yasmeen's house right now, pick up Fatimah, and try to straighten out the mess that I've made!"

"I think that's a terrific idea, Jennah!" Sister Iman said. "But, hold on a minute... there's something I want to give you before you go that might help you out. Keep it in a safe place and read it when you feel that you're ready to make a change. You know, I think that one of the hardest parts of growing up is admitting that you've made a mistake and then trying to fix that mistake."

I gave Sister Iman a big smile and then hugged her tightly. The few minutes I had spent with her seemed to clear my head of all my anger and jealousy. I realized now how silly I had been acting and I felt very grown up as I said *salam* and headed towards the door.

"Wait a minute, Jennah," Sister Iman called after me as I was about to leave. "Here, keep these with you." She handed me a few squares of paper with some writing on them. I glanced down at them quickly and shoved them deep into my pocket to read later on, since I couldn't wait to get back to Yasmeen's house and talk to my friends first.

As I turned to walk out of the door, I bumped right into a very tall, and full-bearded man who was busy talking to a skinny boy with a baseball cap on his head.

"Oh, Brother Yousef!" I exclaimed to the older man. "I'm sorry. I didn't see you coming in."

"*As-salamu 'alaikum*, little Jennah," he answered. "I not see you here in long long time ago. I so happy to see you again. Come stay and sit some."

Brother Yousef always made me giggle when he tried so hard to speak proper English in his broken Syrian accent.

As I smiled up at Sister Iman's husband, I realized that the boy standing next to him was Adam, his annoying fourteen year-old nephew who came to visit every summer.

"Hey, watch where you're going chub-a-lub!" Adam called out with his usual rudeness.

Even though Adam has made fun of me for as long as I can remember, he still knows exactly what to say to make my anger really bubble over. Usually, I get so mad at him that I wind up yelling and calling him really mean names that just make him laugh and make me feel terrible afterwards.

Just as I was about to tell him off, I looked over at Sister Iman and remembered what we had just talked about. I took a deep breath and tried very hard to smile back at the obnoxious teenager.

"Oh, Adam," I said sweetly. "*As-salamu 'alaikum*. I didn't really recognize you with that clean shirt on. It's so nice to see you again."

As I watched Adam's mouth drop open in surprise at my

unexpected reply, I couldn't believe how good it felt to have said something nice in return for something mean.

Feeling very proud of myself, I turned to Brother Yousef and said, "I'd love to stay Brother, but I have to go pick up Fatimah before *maghrib* time. Anyway, *jazaki-Allah khair* Sister Iman... I'm sure I won't forget what you told me."

I winked shyly at Sister Iman and waved back while skipping down the steps as fast as I could. I couldn't wait to go talk to everyone again and show them the "new" me.

CHAPTER

4

I looked down at my watch as I stepped out the door and couldn't believe how quickly the half-hour had passed while I was sitting with Sister Iman. Although she hadn't really told me anything I didn't already know, I felt so much better after talking to her, and explaining how I felt. When I had gotten angry at the girls, I hadn't realized that there really wasn't anything to get angry about and that I had actually been mad at Mariam before I even met her. I guess it was like Sister Iman said, jealousy really is a terrible thing that can, like, totally ruin friendships.

Within minutes, I found myself back on Yasmeen's front step ringing the doorbell once again.

"I geeeeeet it! I geeeeeeet it! ME! ME! ME!"

Of course, I knew right away that that screeching voice had to belong to Fatimah. She was the only person I knew that would be willing to commit murder for the sake of answering the telephone or opening the door.

"Oh! Jen-dah! Jen-dah! I miss you, Jen-dah!" She shrieked.

As soon as the door swung open, my little sister threw herself at me and clung to my leg like she hadn't seen me for years. As I tried to untangle her from my leg, I noticed that, as usual, Fatimah's face was scrubby with dirt and cookies, and the clothes she'd borrowed from Mona were hanging off of her little body like dress-up clothes. Still, something about the look of honest love on her face made me laugh.

Because of the good mood I was in, I even bent down and kissed her forehead, (which of course was a big mistake since now I had the grub from her face all over my lips).

"Okay, Fatimah, I missed you too. But, go get your toys now, or whatever else you brought with you, because we have to get ready to go home," I told her as I patted her on the behind to get her moving.

"No! No! No! I stay here at Meen's house! Jen-dah go home... not Fa-tee-ma!" The little monkey screeched as she ran off on her short little legs to grumble and pout under the dining room table, where I guess she thought I wouldn't be able to find her.

I decided to worry about getting Fatimah home later since I was used to her making a scene before leaving Yasmeen's house. Anyway, I figured I had more important things to do first.

I found Yasmeen's mom standing in the kitchen crying from the onions she was chopping for dinner. *"As-salamu 'alaikum,"* I called into the kitchen over the noise of the dishwasher.

"Oh, Jennah. There you are," Yasmen's mom said with a sigh of relief. "I was worried about you. You ran out of here so fast that I figured either you didn't like the smell of the tuna sandwiches I was making, or you forgot we had a bathroom inside the house, and decided to use the bushes instead."

The big smile on her face showed me that Yasmeen's mom was only kidding. I sometimes had a hard time knowing when she was serious and when she was joking. It turns out most of the time she's joking.

I laughed at the joke, and went up to hug her. "I'm sorry. I really shouldn't have run out like that without saying *salam*. But, I was upset about something and felt like I had to leave.

I know it was wrong of me so I came back to apologize to you and the rest of the girls."

"Well, Jennah, you're all friends, and I'm sure friends are allowed to get upset with each other sometimes," she said. "After all, we're all Muslims, and we should try to make excuses for each other before thinking that someone purposely did something hurtful. I'm sure that all you girls always try to do that for each other, since you have such a beautiful friendship."

I felt a little guilty listening to Yasmeen's mom, because I really hadn't made excuses for anyone. I had jumped straight to the conclusion that Yasmeen was looking for a new best friend and that Mariam was trying to take my place. I turned around and started heading upstairs, towards Yasmeen's bedroom. I called to her mom over my shoulder, "Is it okay if I go upstairs to talk to the girls quickly before I take Fatimah and go home?"

"Sure, go right up, dear. But, I think Mariam, Khadija, and Rahma all left right after you did. I'm sure you'll find Yasmeen up there, though," she called after me.

Oh, no! I thought to myself. Now I can't apologize to everyone. I bounded up the stairs anyway, since I knew I could at least talk to Yasmeen.

I knocked on Yasmeen's door at the top of the stairs, "Come in, Mona. The door's open," she called out.

As soon as I walked into the room, Yasmeen dropped the book she was reading in surprise and gave me a huge smile.

Well, at least she looked like she was really glad to see me.

"Jennah! I knew you'd come back, and you wouldn't stay mad at me for long. I was just thinking about bringing Fatimah back to your house so that I could get a chance to talk to you," she said with a sweet smile that brightened up the room like a thousand light bulbs.

"Me... mad at you?" I said in surprise. "You're the one who should be mad at me for the awful way that I treated everyone today!"

Yasmeen raised her eyebrows and answered quietly, "Well, I thought that I must've done something mean to get you so angry like that, and for you to run out of here so quickly."

"No, Yasmeen, it wasn't you at all, it was just me," I said. "See, it was really dumb of me, but when I met Mariam, I got really jealous because you were so excited about being in the same school as her, and everyone was so happy to meet her. I felt really left out."

I stopped for a second, and then continued, "Mariam is so pretty and so nice that I got annoyed because I just knew that you would like her more than me, and that you'd probably want her to be your new best friend. I know that's really silly of me because you can be friends with whoever you want to be friends with, but still, I guess I just acted like a baby about it. When you first told me about Mariam I was kind of hoping that she'd be really ugly and really mean so that it would be easy for everyone to hate her... that's a really terrible thing to think, isn't it?" I sighed.

I sat down on the bed next to Yasmeen and waited for her to say something.

After what seemed to be forever, Yasmeen finally answered me, "Wow." She stopped and took a deep breath. "I never knew you felt that way, Jennah. But, you should know by now that you're more than just a best friend to me...you're like my sister. Honestly, I really like Mariam, and I think that if you give her a chance you'll really like her too. I know that you're a nice person, Jennah, and would never want to hurt someone's feelings. If you just talk to Mariam and give her a chance you're definitely going to love her like a sister too. We all could have a terrific time with our BFF club!"

Yasmeen scooted over on the bed and gave me a big hug, which I thought was kind of corny because I'm not really big on the whole "touchy-feely" thing with my friends. But, I knew that Yasmeen always tried to look at the bright side of any situation and I was sure that what she said made a lot of sense.

"Alright, well, the one thing I have to do now before going home is give Mariam a quick call and apologize for being mean to her. Do you mind if I use your phone?" I asked.

"Of course not! Go ahead," Yasmeen answered happily. "I'll wait for you downstairs and try to get Fatimah ready to go home. Mariam's phone number is written in my phone book right next to the bed."

Yasmeen was absolutely beaming because she was so excited that I was going to try to become friends with Mariam. She hated it whenever any two people were mad at each other for long.

As Yasmeen closed the door behind her, I settled onto the bed and found Mariam's number written in her very organized phone book. I took a deep breath and dialed. Mariam answered on the second ring, *"As-salamu 'alaikum."*

"Wa 'alaikum as-salam. Hey, Mariam! It's me, Jennah," I said.

I waited a few seconds for Mariam to slam the phone down and hang up on me, since I knew that I deserved even more than that. But, I could still hear her breathing on the other end, which was a good sign.

I paused for another second and then rushed on, "I know you probably hate me right now because I was so mean to you, but I just wanted to say I'm sorry, and that I feel really bad about the things I said. I wish there was some way that I could take my words back, because I'm sure you were really hurt by them. I can totally understand if you never want to talk to me again, but I was hoping you'd forgive me for being such a big baby."

I silently prayed to Allah that Mariam would say she wasn't mad at me anymore, and that we could start all over again at being friends. *Al-hamdu-lilah,* my quick *dua'* was answered right away with Mariam's answer, "Cool!" She exclaimed. "You know, I was really hoping that you would call. I really, like, don't even want to talk about what happened before. I'm just so happy that you don't absolutely hate me!"

For the second time today I was surprised by one of my friend's comments. "Of course I don't hate you. I mean I barely even know you. But, what I do know of you, I think I'm really starting to like a lot!" I said with a large amount of enthusiasm.

"Okay, well then let's start over again. My name is Mariam and I just moved here and I'd love to join The BFF Sisters because all the girls in the club are just the type of people I would love to be friends with," Mariam giggled.

"Well, my name is Jennah, and I have a major attitude problem sometimes that I'm trying really hard to control." Mariam and I both started to crack up at how silly our "new" introductions were.

After giggling some more about a bunch of other corny jokes, I looked down at my watch and realized that I had to be home before Mamma would get worried again.

"Oh, Mariam. I hate to hang up on you like this, but I didn't realize what time it is and now I have to get home really quickly."

"Sure, no problem. I'm just really happy that I finally got a chance to talk to you for real, and I'm sure that we're going to wind up being really good friends, *insha'Allah*. I guess I'll see you at the next club meeting," Mariam answered happily.

Then I got another great idea. "You know what, Mariam? Since we decided to have the meetings on Fridays after *salat al-jum'aa*, why don't I come over before prayer *insha'Allah* and we can go to the mosque together? Then we can walk back to Yasmeen's house for the meeting. That way you can see where the *masjid* is and meet some more people. You'll especially love Sister Iman, who I'm sure will be there, *insha'Allah.*"

"Oh, that's a great idea, Jennah!" Mariam gushed. "I'm so happy I think I could cry."

"Yekh! I think I'm gonna' be sick. Please don't get all mushy on me now. I think I've had enough yucky togetherness for today," I joked. "Well, I gotta' go now so I'll see you on Friday, *insha'Allah.* Don't forget!"

"*Jazaki-Allah khair*! Thank you so so so much, Jennah! You just made my day. I really think I'm going to like living here!"

I quickly said *"As-salamu 'alaikum,"* and hung up the phone because Mariam's excitement was making me a little embarrassed.

Whistling, I jogged down the steps, and braced myself for the big battle of dragging Fatimah home before it got dark out.

CHAPTER

5

I couldn't believe that it was already Friday morning and I hadn't even started researching my *hadeeth* yet for today's meeting. All week, I had been busy talking to the girls, helping at the Muslim day camp and hanging out with Mariam.

Even though I knew that I had wanted to become friends with Mariam, I didn't realize how much we had in common and how much fun she could be.

Now, after wasting the whole week, I was in a real panic now because I had made such a big deal about doing the first *hadeeth* and now I was so unprepared.

I sat at the kitchen table with a thousand books spread in front of me and absolutely no idea where to begin. I had only a few hours left before it was time to go to the first, official, BFF Sisters meeting. Mamma was sorting out the laundry in the other room while Fatimah was running around her in circles, pretending to help.

I tried to concentrate as much as I could on the books in front of me, but I felt like I would never be able to find the perfect *hadeeth* for the first meeting. Just as I was about to give up on my own efforts, and ask my mom for help, she called me into the laundry room.

When I dragged my feet into the other room to see what I could help Mamma with, she said, "Jennah, dear, I found these papers in the pocket of your jeans. Did you need them?"

I looked down at the crumpled squares of paper in my mom's hands and tried to remember where they came from. Then, all of a sudden, I remembered. I reached down and opened one of the squares of paper that I had carelessly shoved in my pocket before leaving Sister Iman's house.

"YES! YES! YES! *Al-hamdu-lilah*! I am soooo happy! Mamma, you're the best for finding these...and Sister Iman is the best for giving them to me! YES! YES! YES!" I screamed as I started following Fatimah in her little dance around the laundry room.

I was so happy that the papers were actually short little *hadeeths* that Sister Iman had wanted me to read. I was a hundred percent sure that they would be just perfect for the meeting today. I bent down and kissed Mamma's cheek before running back to my spot at the kitchen table.

"Well, if I knew that a little piece of paper tucked into your pants could make you that happy, I would always surprise you with paper from the laundry," my mom said.

Mamma smiled at me to see how happy I was, and Fatimah came running after me into the kitchen thinking that the shouting and dancing around that I was doing was some new game that she could join in.

"Oh, no you don't, Fatimah. Go back and help Mamma with the laundry because I've got a ton of work that I have to do right now."

I felt very important telling Fatimah that I had work to do when it wasn't even homework or something that a teacher had told me to do.

"I want help toooo," wailed Fatimah. "Fa-tee-ma be good girl. I pe-rah-meese. Puh-leeeeeeeze Jen-dah. Puh-leeeeeeeeze!"

I could just sense a temper-tantrum about to happen so I knelt down to Fatimah's level, and whispered in her ear, "If you go help Mamma with the laundry now, at night, insha'Allah, I'm going to give you a big surprise. But, it's a secret that you can't tell anyone... okay?" I whispered, as Fatimah's eyes opened wide at the idea of getting a big, secret surprise.

"O-tay!" Fatimah agreed with sparkling eyes, and went running back to the laundry room. I figured I'd worry about coming up with a surprise for her a little later on.

I settled myself back into my chair and began reading the little pieces of paper that Sister Iman had given me. Just like I thought, there were several sayings of the Prophet Muhammed (pbuh) that applied exactly to the way I had acted last week at Yasmeen's house.

After reading all the different *hadeeths*, I finally decided on the perfect one that I figured would be the best way to start off our meetings.

Just as I was finishing up what I would say at the meeting, I realized that it was almost time for the Friday prayer. I gathered up all my books and tucked my notes into a little notebook that I thought we could all use at our meetings. I jogged up the stairs and ran into the bathroom before Fatimah could have a chance to follow me. I clipped my nails, bathed, made *wudu'*, brushed my teeth and put on my scarf so that I would be all clean for s*alat al-jum'aa.*

I skipped into the living room and said, "If it's okay with you, Mamma, I wanted to go pick up Mariam and go to the *masjid* for *salah* and then to Yasmeen's house for a little while. Then I'll come right home, *insha'Allah.*"

"Sure, sweetie go right ahead," Mamma answered. "Actually, if I can settle Fatimah down for a nap, I might actually bring her in the stroller to the *masjid*, too, since I know that's the only way she'll keep quiet during the *khutba.*"

I realized too late that I had forgotten to lower my voice while talking to Mamma and that Fatimah had heard me say I was going to Yasmeen's house. Just as I had expected, my little sister started to wail.

"No nap! No nap! No nap!" Fatimah started stomping around us in a circle while screeching, "I go wid Jen-dah, not wid Mamma!"

Mamma motioned for me to slip out while I still could. I felt bad leaving her to deal with the little monster, but I didn't want to be late for the prayer. So, as quietly as I could, I inched my way out of the house and closed the door behind me on Fatimah's constant chanting.

When I reached Mariam's house, I found her waiting outside for me on her front step. Her beautiful hair was pulled back and covered by a very silky, and very grown-up kind of scarf. Mariam was dressed up in a pretty *gilbab* with Palestinian designs all over it. Looking at how nice and fancy Mariam looked, I wished that I had worn something a little less childish than my typical jeans and long-sleeved T-shirt with a two-piece cotton scarf on my head.

Because I was analyzing the way Mariam was dressed, I didn't even notice the big smile she had on her face, and the way she was actually glowing to see me. When I finally did look up, I realized how good it felt to have a friend who was really that happy to see me.

"*As-salamu 'alaikum.* Hey, Mariam! You look really nice today, *masha'Allah.* That's a really beautiful scarf," I said. I figured the least I could do was control my jealousy before it even started, and make sure that I erased any mean thoughts right away.

"*Jazaki-Allah khair,* Jennah. I'm so happy to see you. You look good too. You look like you're dressed really comfortably. My mom made me get dressed up since she says you have to look nice when you go to pray *salat al-jum'aa.*"

"Yeah, I know. My mom says the same thing. But, a new pair of jeans and a clean long-sleeved T-shirt is about as fancy as I can get. Anyway, you wanna' get going so we won't be late, *insha'Allah?*"

As Mariam hopped off her front steps, I noticed that she was wearing a colorful friendship bracelet on her wrist that looked like the ones Yasmeen had taught me how to make a few weeks ago.

"Cool bracelet, Mariam. Where'd you get it?" I asked out of curiosity.

"Oh... umm... oh...." Mariam looked down while she quickly tried to hide the bracelet under her sleeve and slowly said, "Well, Yasmeen gave it to me."

"Oh!" I answered.

I smiled back at Mariam and tried really hard not to show how hurt and upset I was. It wasn't easy keeping my mouth shut when I really wanted to tell Mariam how rotten I felt. I just couldn't believe that Yasmeen had given her a friendship bracelet that she had to hide from me.

Even though it was hard for me not to blow up at Mariam, I just bit down on my lower lip and tried not to look too angry. I knew that if I let go of my anger now, Mariam would definitely hate me forever. I decided to just wait and talk to Yasmeen about it when I saw her instead of getting Mariam mad at me again.

"Well, let's get going," I said as calmly as I could.

Mariam looked relieved that I had dropped the subject of the bracelet and quickly followed behind me as we headed towards the *masjid.*

We got there just in time to hear the *adthan* starting. I took off my clunky sneakers and put them right next to Mariam's delicate sandals, and we both slipped quietly into two empty spots right next to Khadija's mom.

The *khutba* was given by Brother Yousef in Arabic, while Rahma's father translated it into English. It was kind of weird that what they discussed was one of the *hadeeths* that Sister Iman had given me to read. It was the *hadeeth* that says, "A man said to the Prophet (pbuh): 'Counsel me.' The Prophet (pbuh) said: 'Do not become angry.' The man repeated [his request] several times, and the Prophet (pbuh) said: 'Do not become angry.'"

Brother Yousef explained the *hadeeth* by saying that a person can't help feeling angry sometimes. But, what the Prophet (pbuh) was trying to say, is that good Muslims should never act on their anger.

I thought about what Brother Yousef was saying and I realized that when I am angry I do really mean things that I normally wouldn't do. It made a lot of sense that instead of forcing myself to not feel angry, I should just try to make sure that I don't act in a bad way when I am mad.

I really love it when Brother Yousef gives the Friday lecture, because everything he says is always so easy to understand and can be used in real life.

As we finished the prayer and people started heading outside, I spotted Yasmeen, Khadija, and Rahma and called out to them, "*As-salamu 'alaikum.* Hey, you guys! Are you ready for the first official meeting of The BFF Sisters?"

Funny as it was, I was already starting to get some butterflies in my stomach because of how excited I was about our meeting. It was strange, but I was also feeling good about the fact that I hadn't said anything to Mariam about the friendship bracelet.

"Well, someone's in a good mood today," Khadija said with a smile.

She was dressed a lot like me, in a clean, comfortable, casual outfit. Rahma and Yasmeen, on the other hand, looked just as dressed-up as Mariam with their colorful *shalwar-kameeze* and matching scarves.

"Now that we're all here, let's go back to my house so we can get started." Yasmeen said with a lot of excitement.

I looked over at Yasmeen as she was talking and noticed that she had a friendship bracelet on that looked just like the one Mariam was wearing. I couldn't believe that the two of them were acting like they were the best of friends.

As we all slipped our shoes on, Mariam pulled Yasmeen aside and started whispering something in her ear. I was so angry! As if it wasn't bad enough that they were exchanging gifts behind my back, but now the two of them were telling each other secrets too!

All the nice feelings that I had started to have towards Mariam were quickly being replaced by mean thoughts. Even though Yasmeen had said she wasn't looking for a new best friend, it sure seemed like she had just found one anyway.

Just as I was about to go over to where they were standing and really go off on Yasmeen and Mariam, Khadija called out after me.

"Jennah, why don't you guys go on ahead of me and I'll meet you there. There's something that I need to do first so I'll catch you all later," Khadija said quickly as she took off in the opposite direction.

We all looked at Rahma for an explanation since we figured she knew Khadija best and would know where she was going.

Rahma just shrugged angrily, "Don't ask me what that's all about. She barely even talks to me now. Ever since she met that new girl, Lisa, it's like I don't even exist anymore," she said, walking ahead of us a little so that we wouldn't see the tears in her eyes.

Forgetting my own anger, I sped up my pace a bit and caught up with her, saying, "Hey, Rahma, it's not like you to be all depressed and stuff like that. Come on, I'm sure Khadija just had to run a quick errand or something. Anyway, even though I haven't met Lisa yet, I'm sure she's a good person. You know Khadija doesn't really become friends with just anyone."

"I know, but she's been acting so weird these past couple of days. She acts like she has this big secret that she can't tell me about and all I ever hear now is, 'Lisa did this' and 'Lisa said that.' It's so annoying! I mean if she wants a new best friend, she can just tell me straight up!"

I looked at Rahma with a funny expression on my face. I couldn't believe that the way she was feeling was the exact same way that I had felt about Mariam just a few minutes ago. Listening to Rahma's problem reminded me of how childish I was being.

I knew that I had to tell Rahma the same things that I had needed to hear in order to understand that we were all good friends and that Khadija would never drop her for someone new.

"Why are you looking at me like that, Jennah? Do I have a boogie in my nose or something?"

I laughed at Rahma while she frantically looked for a tissue to wipe her nose.

"No, silly. I was just thinking that the way you feel about Lisa and Khadija is the exact same way I felt about Mariam and Yasmeen. Remember how I exploded at Mariam last week for no reason? Well, it was really because I thought Mariam was trying to take my place and become Yasmeen's new best friend. I was so angry and I just didn't know how to control my anger. So, I acted like a big baby. But, as soon as I gave Mariam a chance, I found out that she's a great person and that with her, Yasmeen and I could have even more fun together. I'm not saying it's easy to feel left out, but I think I learned the hard way that getting angry doesn't help."

As we walked, Rahma kept shaking her head like she wasn't really convinced.

"Yeah, but Mariam really is a nice person. And at least Mariam is Muslim. Lisa's not even Muslim," Rahma whispered it as if she was saying something dirty.

"Rahma, c'mon don't be like that. You should try to look at the bright side of everything," I answered in surprise. "I mean think of Khadija's parents before they became Muslim. If your parents had decided not to become friends with them just because they weren't Muslim, well, then they might have thought that Muslims were stuck up. They might never have become Muslim and we may never have even become friends with Khadija."

I was starting to feel pretty proud of myself because I could see Rahma actually considering what I was saying. I wasn't even that annoyed at Mariam and Yasmeen anymore for whispering to each other or exchanging friendship bracelets.

"Okay, I guess you're right," Rahma finally agreed. "But, if I don't like her, I am not going to become friends with this new girl just because Khadija thinks she's so great."

"Fair enough…just as long as you give her a chance. Okay?" I asked.

I could tell that Rahma was feeling a little better now after our talk, and I just hoped that she wouldn't be mean to Lisa when she first met her the way I acted with Mariam.

By the time I finished my conversation with Rahma, we had already reached Yasmeen's house, and were heading up the stairs towards her room.

CHAPTER

6

We had all been sitting for almost a half-hour in Yasmeen's room, just watching the clock and waiting for Khadija to come. Finally, I felt like I couldn't wait any longer.

"You know what guys?" I said, "We should just start because we can't always wait for one person who's going to be late all the time. Our meetings have to start on time if we're going to take them seriously, okay?"

Rahma was quick to agree with me because I could tell she was still annoyed at Khadija. Yasmeen was unsure at first but then changed her mind after waiting hopelessly for a few more minutes.

I took a deep breath and said, "*Bismillah*" before starting. "Well, the *hadeeth* that I chose to do today has to do with the mean way I acted last time we were here. First, I'll read the *hadeeth* and then I guess we can talk about it."

I took another deep breath and began reading from my notes, "The Prophet (pbuh) was asked: 'What is the person that can be the best friend?'

'He who helps you when you remember Allah, and he who reminds you when you forget Him,' he replied.

Then he, peace be upon him, was asked: 'And which friend is the worst?'

'He who does not help you when you remember Allah and does not remind you of Allah when you forget,' he replied.

Then he was asked: 'Who is the best among people?'

He replied: 'He who, when you look at him, you remember Allah.'"

Everyone kind of sat quietly thinking about what I had said after I finished reading the *hadeeth*, and I decided to be the first one to break the ice and tell my friends what I thought of when I first read it.

"See, when I read this, I realized that our club is really the best idea that we ever came up with. Because, instead of getting together and gossiping, or talking about silly things, we'll be talking about Islam and learning new things all the time. I also realized that you all really are my best friends because, by coming together and doing these meetings every week, when we look at each other we really will remember Allah (swt). And we'll be helping each other by reminding each other to do good things and become better Muslims, *insha'Allah*."

Rahma who had been sitting quietly in the corner suddenly spoke up, "Yeah, you're right. And, I guess even if we did become friends with non-Muslims still we could remember Allah (swt) by doing *dawah* and talking to them about Islam. If we set a good example they could even wind up becoming Muslims and helping us even more in doing good things."

When she finished, I winked at Rahma because I knew exactly what and who she was talking about.

Mariam, Yasmeen, Rahma and I kept talking about the *hadeeth* for the next few minutes. In the middle of our discussion the door burst open and in came Khadija.

"*As-salamu 'alaikum.* Sorry I'm late, guys. But the party can get started now that I'm here!" Khadija said, as she shot us all a winning smile.

"What party?" Rahma rolled her eyes sarcastically, "We've already had all the fun and were just leaving when you came in. Nobody even noticed you weren't here."

Khadija's happy expression fell while she listened to Rahma's comments.

I edged closer to Rahma and squeezed her hand trying to remind her of what we had just discussed and to stop her from hurting her best friend like I had. *Al-hamdu-lilah*, Rahma understood right away and broke into a grin.

"Nah, I'm just kidding Khadija. I just wanted to joke around with you a little."

Khadija sighed an exaggerated sigh of relief and held the door open, saying, "Well, now that I know you're not mad at me... there's someone I'd like you to meet." Khadija stepped away from the door and in walked a very tall, and very beautiful, blonde and blue-eyed girl. "This is Lisa. She's new in town and wanted to meet some other people our age so I hope you don't mind Yasmeen, I invited her to stop by...just to meet you guys."

Lisa walked over to Rahma, "You must be Rahma. I've heard so much about you from Khadija that I just couldn't wait to meet you. I think you're even prettier than Khadija said you were."

Rahma rolled her eyes and whispered in my ear, "She's such a kiss-up. I think I'm gonna' puke."

She turned and shot Lisa a very fake and smug smile. But, Lisa didn't seem to notice, and returned a real smile, saying, "You know Rahma, it's so nice that you're Khadija's best friend. You remind me so much of my best friend who still lives in Florida."

Lisa's words seemed to work like a charm on Rahma. Her gloomy expression changed into a full smile as she looked up at Lisa and said in surprise, "You mean...you already have a best friend? So...you're not even looking for a new one?"

Lisa shook her head and laughed. Rahma let out a huge sigh of relief and wiped the mean look off her face completely.

Khadija went around the room introducing Lisa to everyone.

Mariam, of course, was thrilled to find that she wasn't the only new girl in town anymore.

All of us, including Rahma, started to really like Lisa right away. She was so friendly and sweet that we felt like she was already one of the gang. That's when I got another one of my great ideas. I pulled Yasmeen over to the side of the room while the other girls were busy filling Lisa and Khadija in on what we had just been talking about.

I whispered to Yasmeen my idea and she nodded with a big smile and said that it really was a great idea. Then, I went back to the group and said, "Lisa, I know that you may not know that much about Islam yet... and, I know that Rahma and Mariam were just explaining to you about our club... so... I was thinking maybe you'd like to join."

I looked around the room to make sure that everyone agreed. Mariam, Khadija and even Rahma nodded their heads slowly. "Well, I dunno'," Lisa said quietly, "I mean it's really nice of you and all... and I would love to join...but, I'm not Muslim or anything, so I don't want to make you guys feel uncomfortable, you know?"

Lisa looked around the room questioningly at all our expectant faces, then she cracked a big smile and said, "Yes, I'll join. I'd love to be a part of The BFF Sisters. I've learned so much already about Islam from Khadija, and I would love to learn a lot more. I'll try to keep up with you guys and not ask too many silly questions."

Lisa's reaction was exactly what everyone was hoping for. "You know what, I just got an even better idea," I exclaimed jumping up from my seat and stepping on Kit-Cat in my excitement.

As Yasmeen's cat scurried out of her room all the girls giggled and said, "Oh no! Not another great idea!"

I joined in the laughter and said, "No, seriously! Listen, every time we do a *hadeeth*, the person who prepares should write it down with their comments in this notebook. That way, if anyone comes late or doesn't understand something, they can go back to the notebook and look it up without being embarrassed or too shy to ask questions or anything. We can even put definitions in the book or explanations or why we chose the *hadeeth*...anything we feel like putting in there will be cool. Then, you can always come to a meeting early, or stay a little late to read the notebook. And, every week, the person who prepares will take the notebook home to write her *hadeeth* in it."

I ran out of breath since I was talking so quickly the way I usually do when I'm excited about something.

"Surprisingly, that really is a good idea," Mariam joked.

"Okay, I think we might hurt ourselves with all these good ideas floating around, so why don't we take a break and find something good to eat in the kitchen downstairs?" Khadija said.

"Wait a second, you guys," Yasmeen answered. "Mariam and I have a surprise for everyone."

Yasmeen reached under her bed and pulled out a little bag while Mariam grinned back at us. I just rolled my eyes at the thought of the two of them sharing another secret.

As Yasmeen opened the bag, Mariam said, "See, we thought it would be nice to make friendship bracelets for everyone in the club. We figured that it could be like our secret code or something and we'd have to wear them all the time."

Yasmeen continued excitedly, "We took some of our allowance money and bought the string and beads and stuff and made these cool bracelets for everyone. We even made an extra one which will be just perfect for you, Lisa."

Wow! I thought to myself. So, this was the reason why Yasmeen and Mariam were whispering before.

"That's really nice of you guys," I said. "You know when I first saw you two wearing the bracelets, I got really angry. Although it really wasn't easy for me to control my anger, I can only say *al-hamdu-lillah* that I didn't explode and act like a baby again. Boy, do I feel stupid for thinking the worst about my closest friends."

Yasmeen looked over at me and smiled as she reached into the bag and pulled out a beautiful pink bracelet.

"Here you go, Jennah. I made this one especially for you because I know how much you love the color pink," she said.

I looked around the room at all my old friends and my new ones, too. I felt really good about the way things had turned out, and I was sure that everything was just going to get better and better.

"Well, you know, this is all great and jolly and all but can we please go get something to eat now because I am starving," Khadija said.

We all laughed at Khadija, and headed downstairs to search for some junk food.

CHAPTER

7

A few hours later, I was heading home with a very happy feeling in my stomach. We had decided that Khadija should do the next *hadeeth* because she was late this time, but she surprised us all by saying that she was leaving next week to do *umra* in Saudi Arabia. Since this will be Khadija's first time ever going anywhere outside of the United States, she's real excited. Actually, we're all really excited for her because Khadija's never even been on an airplane. Oh, and Rahma, of course, was real happy to find out that this was the big secret that Khadija had wanted to surprise us all with. So, by the end of the meeting, we all decided to just take turns doing the *hadeeths* until Khadija came back from her trip.

As I skipped towards my house and thought about how great The BFF Sisters Club was going to be, I noticed a strange car in our driveway. All of a sudden, I realized whose car it had to be. I stopped for a second and then began racing all the way home. I ran up the front steps and opened the door calling out, "Baba! Baba!"

Sure enough, just as I had guessed, my father stood in the doorway with his arms wide open just waiting to hug me.

"Surprise, little Jennah! Did you miss me?" He asked as I ran into his arms and squeezed him as tight as I could.

"Baba! I didn't know you were coming today. I'm so happy you're here! I missed you sooooo much! Why didn't you tell me you were coming? I would've stayed home today and waited for you!" I said breathlessly.

"Whoa...slow down a little, *batata.*"

I giggled at the funny nickname, which means 'sweet potato,' that Baba always calls me by. "Well, I missed all three of my beautiful girls, as well as the baby on the way, so I couldn't wait any longer to come home. If I told you all I was coming today, it wouldn't be a surprise, now would it?"

Mamma came waddling into the kitchen behind Baba with the happiest expression on her face. I smiled to see how excited Mamma was to have Baba back. Just as I was thinking to myself that the house was nice and quiet and peaceful now that Baba was home, Fatimah came bounding into the kitchen and all of a sudden threw herself at me.

As I tried to pick myself up off of the floor, Fatimah began screeching, "Jen-dah, Jen-dah! Dis da good suprize you tell me 'bout. I wuv dis suprize. Tank you Jen-dah for bwinging Baba back," gushed Fatimah as she practically strangled me with another one of her enthusiastic hugs.

I couldn't help laughing at Fatimah's way of thinking and I figured it wouldn't really hurt for me to take a little credit for the surprise.

Mamma and Baba joined in the laughter. Then Baba said to us, "Hurry up, girls and wash up for dinner so that I can show you all the nice things I brought back for you. Then, if you finish up all your dinner, we can go down to the Point Pleasant amusement park and spend some time together on the boardwalk."

Fatimah, of course, had no trouble understanding the words "amusement park" and raced to the kitchen sink, where Mamma helped her wash her hands, and sat her down in her high chair.

I have to admit that even I was almost as excited as Fatimah was that finally things could go back to normal around here, at least for a little while anyway. Even Mamma's Egyptian food tasted as good as pizza today because Baba was with us.

After dinner, Baba surprised us all again by saying, "I've decided that all this travelling makes me very lonely because I miss you all very much when I'm gone. And, with the new baby coming, it will be very hard for your mom to be by herself all the time."

Baba looked over at Mamma and shared a secret smile and a little wink with her before going on, "So, I've decided to change jobs, and take a position that I won't need to travel for anymore."

I couldn't believe what I was hearing. Ever since I was Fatimah's age, Baba's always been gone on far-away trips, now I was finally going to have a normal family like all my friends.

Baba continued what he was saying, "Even though the new job pays a little less, we'll just have to be kind of careful on how much we spend all the time. At least, *al-hamdu-lilah*, we'll all be together though."

I was so happy to hear what Baba was saying that I jumped out of my chair and gave him another huge hug. Fatimah, who didn't really understand what was going on, wanted to make sure that no one had forgotten about her by throwing her peas and carrots all across the room.

"Okay, everyone," Mamma called out over Fatimah's very loud and off key singing of 'The Itsy-Bitsy Spider,' "I think it's time to clean up and start heading out before it gets too late."

Baba agreed with Mamma and joined in cleaning up, while I grabbed Fatimah and headed upstairs with her to try and calm her excitement down a little bit, while I changed her clothes.

I realized that even Fatimah's mess seemed kind of cute today. After all, with all the wonderful things that had happened to me, I couldn't stop smiling and saying, "*Al-hamdu-lilah. Al-hamdu-lilah* for my family and my friends and even The BFF Sisters club."

THE OFFICIAL BFF SISTERS NOTEBOOK

July 10,

Okay, guys. I'm going to be the first one to write in this notebook because I know you all think it's cheezy, but I think it's important.

The *hadeeth* that I chose to do was actually one that Sister Iman gave me. Like I said before, it was really important because it reminded me of what true friendship is all about.

I think our club is great because all of us are true friends even according to the Islamic definition since we all remind each other to do good things.

Well, that was all I really wanted to say and I gotta' go home now anyway so I guess I'll see you all at the next meeting, *insha'Allah*. Oh, by the way, I think I might add a little dictionary to this notebook of some words that I think we should all know.

Sorry, I don't mean to sound bossy again... but, if we want to learn we should probably do it right... at least that's something that Sister Iman always says. Salamz for now,

Jennah

OUR DICTIONARY

Adthan
The Muslim call to prayer which is made before each *salah.*

Allah (swt)
The Arabic name for God, the One and Only. The (swt) which always follows stands for the Arabic words *"Subhanahu wa Ta'ala"* which mean "All Praise and Glory belong to Him."

Al-hamdu-lilah
Praise and thanks be to Allah.

As-salamu 'alaikum
The proper Muslim greeting and farewell which means "Peace be upon you."

As-staghfur Allah Al-'atheem
A *dua'* which means "I seek refuge from Allah, the Almighty."

Bismillah
In the name of Allah. This is what Muslims should say before beginning anything they do in life.

Dawah
This is the process of teaching others about Islam.

Dua'
When one prays to Allah for anything good in this life or the next.

Gilbab
A long dress that is very loose and covers the whole body.

Hadeeth
The sayings and actions of the Prophet (pbuh) which we should always try to follow.

Hijab
The proper Islamic dress for a Muslim woman after the age of puberty which covers everything except the face and the hands.

Iftar
Breaking the fast at sunset.

Insha'Allah
If Allah is willing. This is something Muslims should always say whenever they speak about the future.

Jazaki-Allah khair
May Allah reward you with good. This is what Muslims should say to each other when they interact with one another.

Khutba
The Friday lecture before *salat al-jum'aa.*

Masha'Allah
This means "what Allah has willed" and should be said whenever someone sees something beautiful or speaks about something very good.

Masjid
This is the Arabic term for a Muslim place of worship (mosque).

Prophet (pbuh)
This refers to the Prophet Muhammed, the Last Messenger of Allah (swt). The (pbuh) which always comes after it stands for "peace and blessings of Allah be upon him."

Qur'an
The Muslim Holy Book which was revealed to the Prophet Muhammed (pbuh) through the Angel *Gibreel*.

Ramadan
Holy month in which Muslims fast from sunrise to sunset every day because this is the month during which the Qur'an was revealed.

Sabr
The Arabic word for "patience."

Salat al-'asr
The afternoon prayer.

Salat al-dhuhr
The noon-time prayer.

Salat al-fajr
The sunrise prayer.

Salat al-jum'aa
The Friday prayer.

Salat al-maghrib
The sunset prayer.

Shalwar-kameeze
Pakistani dress which works well with *hijab*.

Shaytan
The Arabic word for "the devil" or another word for "*Iblis*."

Surah
A chapter of the Qur'an which is made up of smaller verses.

Umra
The religious pilgrimage and visit to Makkah in Saudi Arabia.

Wa 'alaikum as-salam
The proper Islamic greeting and farewell response which means and peace be unto you too.

Wudu'
The cleansing of the body in preparation for prayer.

WHAT SOME OF OUR ARABIC NAMES MEAN

Jennah (Jen-nah)
Arabic word for Heaven.

Yasmeen (Yes-meen)
Arabic word for the flower, jasmine.

Khadija (Kha-dee-jah)
The name of the Prophet's (pbuh) first wife.

Rahma (Ra-H-mah)
Arabic word for mercy.

Mariam (Ma-ree-yam)
The name of Prophet 'Isa's (pbuh) mother.

Iman (Ee-man)
Arabic word for faith.

Yousef (You-seff)
The name of one of the prophets.

Fatimah (Fa-tee-mah)
The name of the Prophet's (pbuh) daughter.

Bilal (Bee-lal)
The name of the first man to make *adthan* during the time of the Prophet (pbuh).

Mustafa (Moo-sta-fah)
Another name for the Prophet (pbuh).

Mona- (Mu-nah)
Comes from the Arabic word which means to hope.